637
MCF

McFarland, Cynthia

Cows in the parlor

$13.95   19095

DATE			

COWS
IN THE PARLOR

COWS
IN THE PARLOR

A Visit to a Dairy Farm

CYNTHIA McFARLAND

ATHENEUM   1990   NEW YORK

Atheneum
Macmillan Publishing Company
866 Third Avenue, New York, NY 10022
Collier Macmillan Canada, Inc.
First Edition
Printed in Singapore
10 9 8 7 6 5 4 3 2 1

Library of Congress Cataloging-in-Publication data
McFarland, Cynthia.
Cows in the parlor.
Summary: Discusses the activities of a dairy farm
and describes a typical day as the cows are fed, milked,
and put away for the night.
1. Dairy farming—Juvenile literature. 2. Dairy
farms—Juvenile literature. [1. Dairy farms. 2. Dairying]
I. Title.
SF239.5.M34 1990 637 89-14972
ISBN 0-689-31584-8

To my friends and family
for their support and encouragement;
and to my mother
for teaching me a love of books
and the written word

Every day is a busy day on Clear Creek Farm. Winter, spring, summer, and fall, the cows on the dairy farm must be milked—twice a day, every day.

When the snow is deep in the fields, and when the hot summer sun shines down on the pastures, the cows need to be milked.

Even on holidays, Charlie Riddle, the farmer, must milk his cows. A dairy cow doesn't have a day off.

Maggie is a Jersey cow. Jerseys are always tan or brown. Some have white spots on their faces and bodies. They are friendly cows and like to be petted.

There are fifty cows on Clear Creek Farm, where Maggie lives. Fancy, Belle, Heather, and Sparkle are some of the other cows' names. It is not easy to think of names for fifty cows.

A tag with a number hangs from the chain around Maggie's neck. Another tag is attached to her ear. When a farmer has many cows, he needs a way to keep track of them. The numbers on the tags help him do this.

The neck chains jingle and rattle when the cows walk or shake their heads.

When the wind is blowing and it is raining or snowing, the cows stay inside the barn. The straw makes a cozy bed when it is cold outside.

When the weather is nice, the cows like to graze in the pasture. The sunshine is warm on Maggie's back as she rests after eating. In the spring and summer when the nights are warmer, the cows sleep outside in the cool grass.

A cow doesn't have top teeth at the front of her mouth as a horse, a dog, or a person does. Maggie has a very long, rough tongue. By wrapping it around the tall grass she can pull off a bite and then chew the grass with her strong back teeth.

In the summer, Mr. Riddle and the farm workers cut grass,

dry it in the sun,

and make it into bales of hay.

The cows will have hay to eat when the grass in the pasture is brown and dry in the winter.

But a cow needs more than grass and hay to make good milk. Charlie Riddle also makes feed from the corn that was planted in the spring.

Machines chop the whole cornstalk into small pieces.

Then the silo is filled with this chopped corn, which is called silage. The silo is very tall. It can hold enough silage to feed the farmer's cows for many months. When snow covers the cornfields, there will still be food for the cows in the silo.

The cows eat their silage at a long trough, called a bunk. Mr. Riddle uses a tractor and feed wagon to take the silage from the silo to the bunk, where the cows are waiting to eat. The cows moo when they see the tractor because they know that soon they will be fed.

Maggie and the other cows know when it is time to be milked because Charlie Riddle and the farm workers milk them at the same time every day. If the cows are out in the field, they start walking up to the barn gate at milking time.

Early in the morning, when most people are asleep in their warm beds, the cows are being milked. In the evening, when most people sit down to eat dinner, the cows must be milked again. At Clear Creek Farm, the Riddle family eats supper earlier in the afternoon, or after the evening milking is finished.

The parlor in a dairy barn is not a pretty living room.
It is the room where the cows are milked.

When Maggie comes in to the parlor, her udder is firm
and full of milk. She stands in a small pen, or stanchion,
and the gates are closed so that she can't leave until she
has been milked. Every time she is milked, her udder is
cleaned and all the dirt is washed off.

Farmers used to milk their cows by hand into a bucket. That took a long time. Now there are automatic milking machines to make the job quicker and easier.

The milking machines don't hurt the cows. Suction from the machines gently pulls the milk from the cows' teats.

utters

The milk runs through shiny silver pipes into a large tank. There the milk is kept cold until it is picked up by the milk hauler.

When the hauler comes, he pumps all the milk into his long tanker truck and takes it to the creamery. There the milk is made into butter, cheese, ice cream, and yogurt. It is also put into cartons so people can pour a glass to drink or have some on their cereal for breakfast. In one day a single cow can give enough milk to fill more than fifty glasses.

To keep making milk, a cow must have a baby every year. Cats and dogs have several babies at a time. A cow usually has only one.

Maggie has just had a calf. The calf is sweet and brown, with large dark eyes like a deer's.

The calf nurses from her mother. That first milk is very important to the baby. It is rich with extra vitamins to keep the newborn calf from getting sick.

After the calf has been with her a day, Maggie will go back into the milking herd. Her calf will live with all the other babies. Each calf has her own small pen bedded with fresh, sweet-smelling straw.

Mr. Riddle feeds them milk from a bottle, and they learn to eat grain from a bucket.

A calf is soft and warm and will suck on the farmer's finger, trying to find milk. She calls "~~maaa maaa~~" to her mom at feeding time.

Calves are frisky and like to play. After running and jumping, they take naps in the sunshine.

A female calf is called a heifer. A male calf is called a bull calf. Charlie Riddle keeps the heifer. Sometimes he sells the bull calves so another farmer can raise them.

Maggie's calf is a heifer. In two years she will be old enough to be bred and have a baby of her own. After she calves, she will be called a cow and will become part of the milking herd just like her mother, Maggie.

After the evening milking, Mr. Riddle finishes his chores. When the parlor is clean, the milking machines and pipes are washed, and the cows are fed, his day's work is done.

The cows finish eating their dinner and lie down to sleep. Soon bright stars glitter in the night sky above the quiet, dark pastures.

When the morning sun comes up again, another busy day will already have begun on Clear Creek Farm.